ALL KINDS OF AWESOME

Jess Hitchman

illustrated by Vivienne To

Feiwel and Friends
New York

Race awesome

Case awesome

Flying into **space** awesome

Making awesome

Baking awesome

What will **you** be?

Art awesome

Chart awesome

Following your **heart** awesome

Living a **big city** life

Or being **wild** and **free**

Show awesome

Grow awesome

Sharing
what you **know**
awesome

Fashion awesome

Passion awesome

Finding time to **play**

Fire awesome

Hire awesome

Helping to **inspire** awesome

Knowing where you want to go

Or **choosing** on the way

Flight awesome

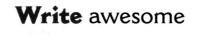

Kissing-them-good-night

awesome

Flying high up in the sky

Or **swimming** in the sea

Find awesome

Kind awesome

Making-up-your-mind

awesome

No matter what,

You'll always be . . .

All kinds of

AWESOME

to me!

Did you know you could turn your awesome passion into an awesome career?

Then you get to do what you love every day.

If your passion is stars and planets, you could be an astronaut who goes to space, an astronomer who studies the night sky, or an aerospace engineer who builds spaceships.

Do you love playing with computer games or robots? Perhaps you could be a coder, inventor, or data scientist. Did you know that lots of people do jobs that didn't even exist when they were growing up? Maybe you'll invent a whole new career, just for you.

Perhaps your superpower is caring for people and animals. If so, you could make an amazing stay-at-home parent, a nurse, or a vet. The world needs more people like you.

Are you happiest when you're playing outdoors? Archaeologists, tree surgeons, and conservationists all work outside whatever the weather. They get to wear some cool outdoor gear, too.

Your passions can be your hobbies as well. Maybe you'll be a lawyer during the day and a ballet dancer by night. Or a deep-sea diver all week and a volunteer firefighter on weekends.

You might do one job your whole life or keep trying out lots of different things. There's no rush in discovering your passions. Just keep exploring and having fun along the way.

For Tabitha —J. H.

For Ellie —V. T.

A Feiwel and Friends Book
An imprint of Macmillan Publishing Group, LLC
120 Broadway, New York, NY 10271

ALL KINDS OF AWESOME. Text copyright © 2021 by Jess Hitchman. Illustrations copyright © 2021 by
Vivienne To. All rights reserved. Printed in China by RR Donnelley Asia Printing Solutions Ltd.,
Dongguan City, Guangdong Province.

Our books may be purchased in bulk for promotional, educational, or business use. Please contact your local
bookseller or the Macmillan Corporate and Premium Sales Department at (800) 221-7945 ext. 5442
or by email at MacmillanSpecialMarkets@macmillan.com.

Library of Congress Cataloging-in-Publication Data is available.
ISBN 978-1-250-24525-0

Book design by Liz Dresner
Feiwel and Friends logo designed by Filomena Tuosto

First edition, 2021
1 3 5 7 9 10 8 6 4 2
mackids.com